MT. PLEASANT BRANCH LIBRARY
VALHALLA, NY

W9-BTL-947

Letters from Space

written by **Clayton Anderson**

Illustrated by **Susan Batori**

Dear Mom:

I did it! I made it into outer space!

LAUNCH WAS SO COOL.

I can't even believe it happened. It was loud, it was scary, and the entire space shuttle shook like crazy. Once we started going really fast, I felt so heavy. It was like I weighed three times what I usually do. We went faster and faster and faster, and then—everything went quiet. I started to rise out of my seat. I was weightless! There's so much more to come. I hope I receive lots of letters during my five months in space.

I love you!

Your son,

Clayton

Hello, Sutton!

Did you see us on TV yet? My head looks ginormous! All the fluids in my body have gone to my head. In weightlessness, that's very common in the first few days. Our hearts pump too much fluid into our heads because our brains think we're still on Earth. But with no gravity, it makes us look like we're a bunch of bobbleheads!

It should go away soon. Our brain and blood-flow systems will figure everything out fast, and I'm hoping I'll look more "normal" very soon.

Keep watching!

Clayton

AL SPACE STATION

L I V E

NEWS

Dear Mission Control:

Just wanted to let you know I'm on day three of my third pair of underwear. I know I'm supposed to wear them for four days before I throw them into the trash. But if they're still pretty clean should I wear them for a few more days? I know we need to conserve our supplies up here!

Thanks!
Clayton

Hey, Cole!

Thanks so much for writing to me! I'm so glad your teacher figured out my address up here. You have a new puppy? That is so cool!

We can't have pets in space. It would be neat to have a dog or a cat, but what a mess with no gravity! Where would it go to the bathroom?!

Astronauts do bring animals to space. There have been mice and spiders and minnows and butterflies. The spiders' webs looked so strange at first—all crooked and messy, but they came around eventually! Astronauts have watched butterflies grow from caterpillars. It took them a while to realize they could still fly. Scientists want to see how animals and insects adapt to being weightless because they might help us figure out how humans adapt to space. Man... human and animal brains are really cool!

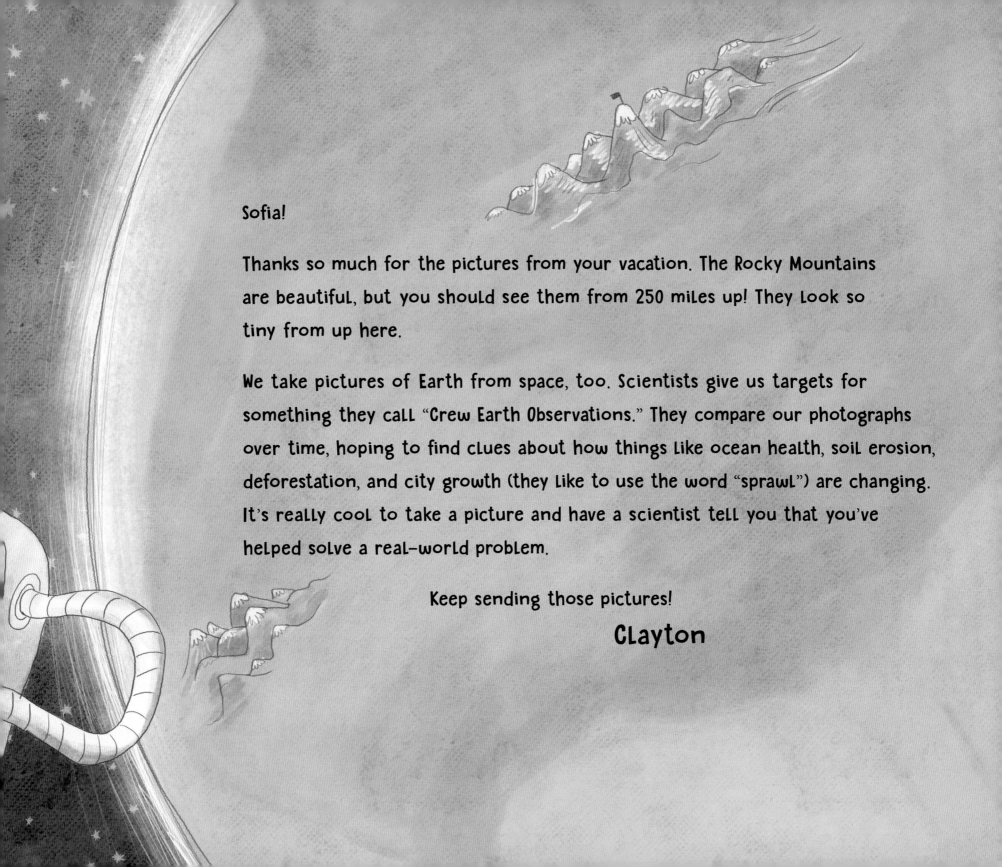

Sofia!

Thanks so much for the pictures from your vacation. The Rocky Mountains are beautiful, but you should see them from 250 miles up! They look so tiny from up here.

We take pictures of Earth from space, too. Scientists give us targets for something they call "Crew Earth Observations." They compare our photographs over time, hoping to find clues about how things like ocean health, soil erosion, deforestation, and city growth (they like to use the word "sprawl") are changing. It's really cool to take a picture and have a scientist tell you that you've helped solve a real-world problem.

Keep sending those pictures!

Clayton

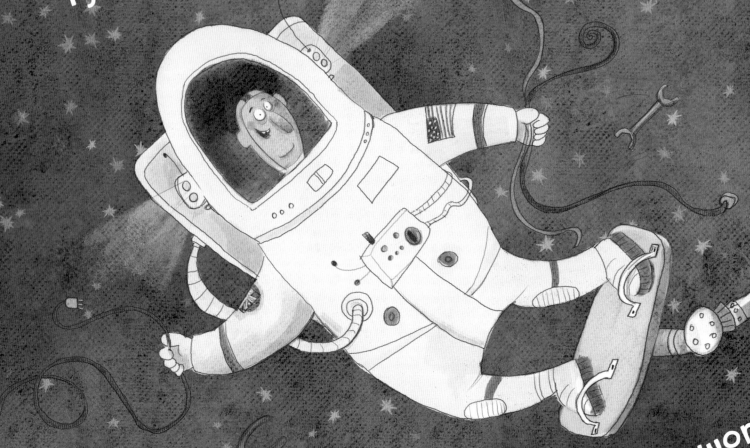

Hello, Brother... I just did a space walk! It was incredible!

I put on my space suit and went outside to work.

In **SPACE!**

When I exited through the hatch, it was totally black outside. The sun was behind the Earth—I couldn't see anything. But I turned my helmet headlights on and went to work.

We were out there for over seven hours and I rode on the robotic arm. I was like one of those guys who fix wires on utility poles. **But in SPACE!** Man, did I have some great views of the Milky Way and the space station!

Spacewalking can really tire you out. It was hard in a thinking kind of way. You must be careful and think about every single thing. Mistakes are bad and we don't get any do-overs!

DANGER

ON

OFF

You'll be happy to know my space suit worked perfectly. It was like I was in my very own personal spaceship. It had everything I needed—oxygen, drinking water, AC—and I could talk to Mission Control. With no gravity, I was flying inside my suit! It was amazing.

See you soon!
Clayton

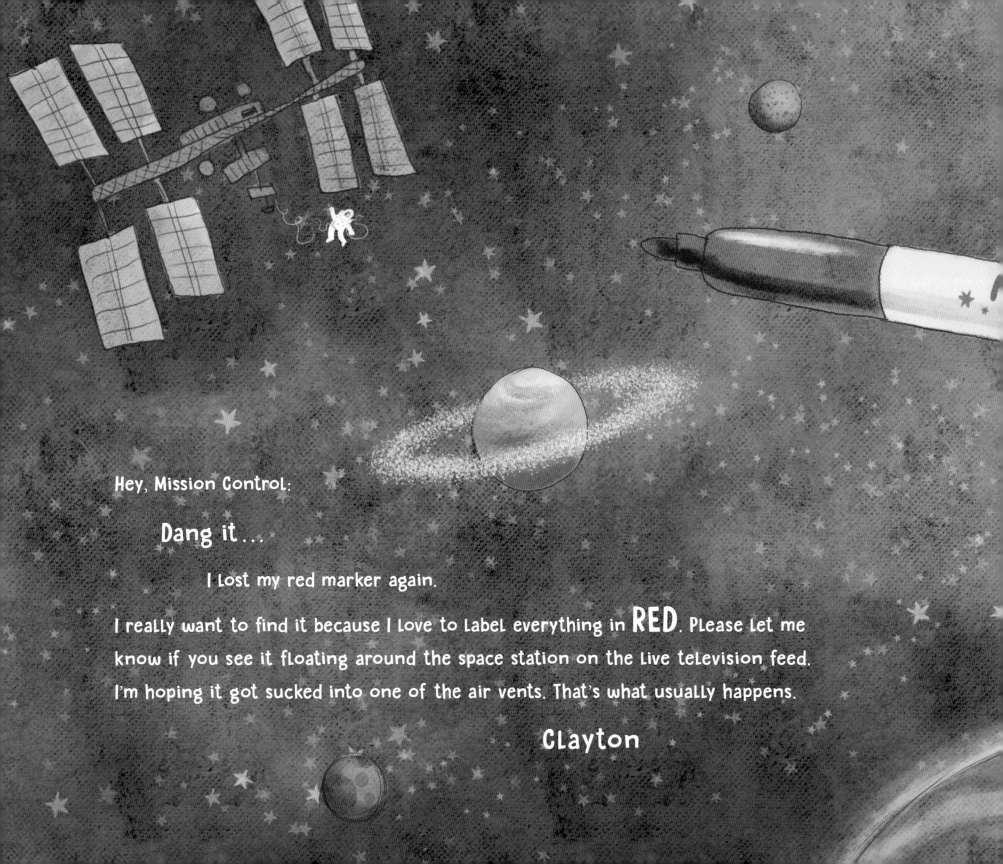

Hey, Mission Control:

Dang it...

I lost my red marker again.

I really want to find it because I love to label everything in **RED**. Please let me know if you see it floating around the space station on the live television feed. I'm hoping it got sucked into one of the air vents. That's what usually happens.

Clayton

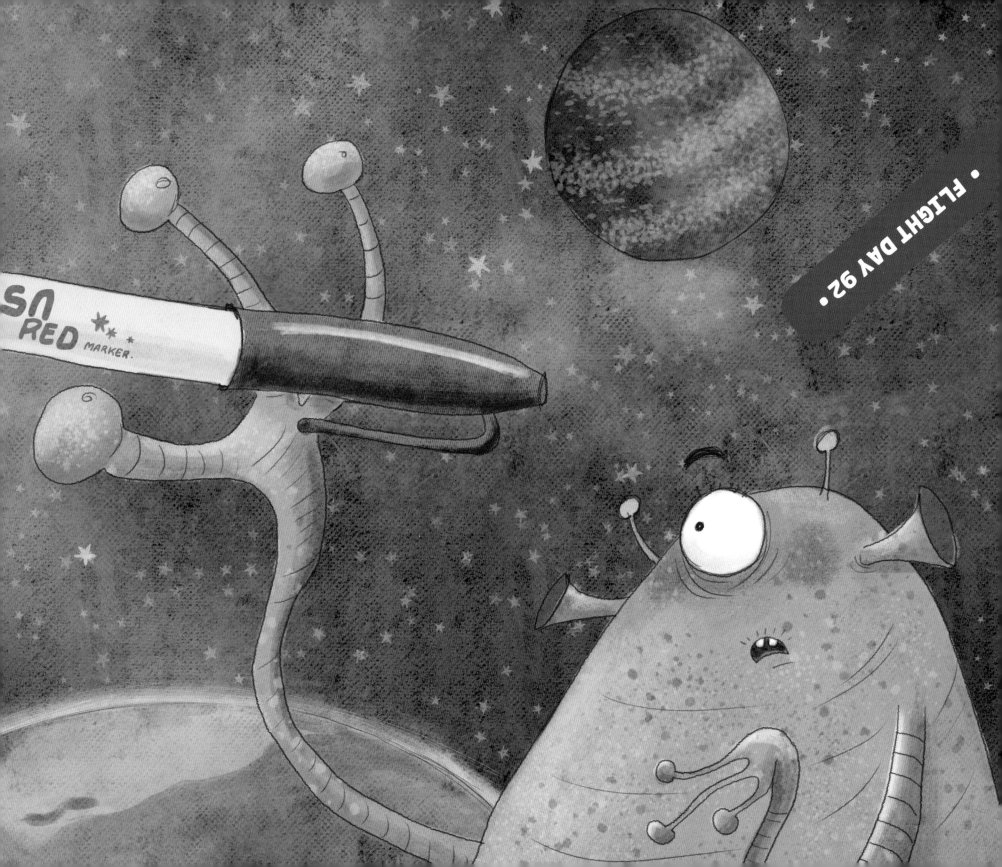

It's lunchtime in space, Ana!

My favorite foods come from Russia. That's a good thing, because my Russian crewmates like all the American food. I love to start my meal with a can of stuff they call "appetizing appetizer." It looks kind of like baby food. Yum. After that, I always love a nice can of lamb with vegetables or pork and potatoes. It looks a lot like cat food. Maybe it even smells like cat food? But I swear it doesn't taste like cat food.

Scientists are watching everything I put in my mouth! I send them notes every week and tell them all the food I ate. They want to know how much I eat, what I eat, and how often I eat! They are trying to figure out what diet will keep us healthy if we stay in space for a long, long time.

Clayton

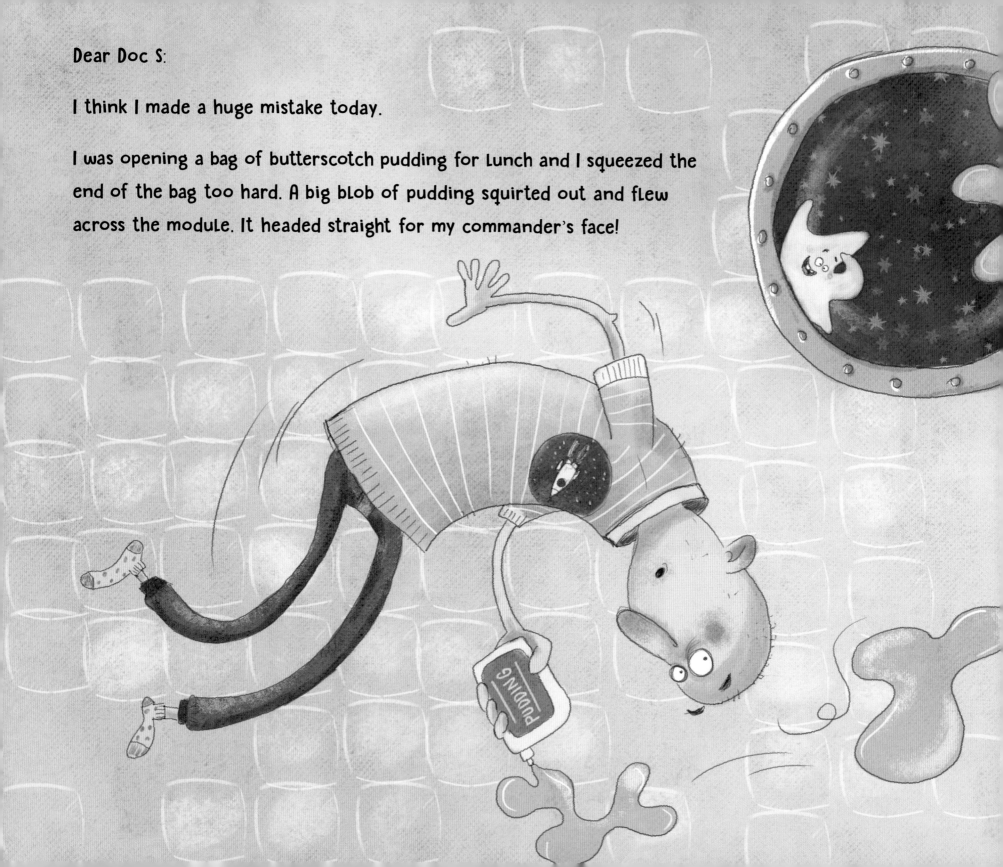

Dear Doc S:

I think I made a huge mistake today.

I was opening a bag of butterscotch pudding for lunch and I squeezed the end of the bag too hard. A big blob of pudding squirted out and flew across the module. It headed straight for my commander's face!

But at the last second he opened his mouth and ate it right out of the air! I was so embarrassed and praying he wouldn't get mad. But he just licked his lips and gave me a thumbs-up. I thought of you because it was a great example of Newton's First Law: "An object either remains at rest or continues to move at a constant velocity, unless acted upon by a force." The pudding was at rest until I acted on the bag with a force!

WHEW... That was a close one.

Clayton

Hey, Tommy!

I was thinking of you today, and how we used to read comic books in Julie's apple tree back home. And then I realized that up here in space, I'm Superman...

...every single day. I fly to breakfast. Then I fly to work. If I need a break, I fly to the bathroom—and I even fly while I'm *going* to the bathroom! So cool!

Stay **SUPER**,
Clayton

Dear Mrs. Raikes:

I know you are nearly halfway through the school year, and I hope your science classes are having fun. I wanted to thank you for teaching me about the scientific method when I was in your class. It made me love science and now I'm doing it in outer space!

We have so many experiments to do while we're in weightlessness. One of my favorites is growing plants. Mission Control sent up two plant-growth chambers on a cargo rocket. One has basil seeds in it and the other has lettuce seeds. I water them every other day and then take photos of them on the days I don't give them water. Kids on Earth are following along to learn how things grow in space. Then they'll design a plant-growth chamber of their own.

Dear Mom:
I'm coming home soon!

I can't wait to give you a huge hug. It has been almost half a year since I launched into space, and I'm looking forward to being home again.

The time has flown by up here (ha ha) and life in weightlessness has been really fun.

I can do so many flips,

I could win an 0lympic gold medal in gymnastics!

I'm ready to feel the sunlight and breeze on my face, and smell freshly cut grass. I'm also ready for a nice big T-bone steak and a baked potato.

I am so proud of everything we've accomplished. I can't believe I did six space walks and flew the robotic arm. Who would have thought a small-town kid would end up living in outer space?

I love you so much... see you soon! Clayton

Dear Mission Control:

I'm home—safely back on Earth. And boy, am I glad about that!

Maybe we should have a big party now that I'm back? We could invite family and friends, and all the great folks who helped keep me safe up there. I know how hard they worked and that they had to spend time away from their families, too. It would be neat to say thank you to them for helping me live my dream.

Respectfully,

Clayton

NASA uses the term Space Adaptation Syndrome (SAS) to describe what happens to astronauts when they first get to space. With no gravity, their bodies are constantly in motion—upside down, sideways, diagonal— and they literally cannot believe their eyes. The brain doesn't understand what the eyes are seeing and astronauts tend to get nauseous. The brain catches up eventually. A good night's sleep helps a lot!

NASA likes to use mice for many of their studies. The life cycle of a mouse is similar to that of a human, but it happens much, much faster. So if we are trying to learn something about humans, mice help us learn sooner. And they're so cute!

NASA astronauts train for space walks in a swimming pool! The pool is 200 feet (61 meters) long, 100 feet (30.5 m) wide, and 40 feet (12 m) deep. It holds 6.2 million gallons (23.5 million liters) of water with a temperature of about 85 degrees Fahrenheit (29.5 degrees Celsius) to keep everyone nice and comfortable.

Astronauts do not have the ability to wash their clothes while in space. They wear each item of clothing longer than we would on Earth, then throw it away. The ground team gives astronauts a recommendation for how long they should wear each item of clothing, like socks, underwear, and t-shirts. But it's just a recommendation—we can wear it as long as we can stand it!

Many astronauts love to take photos of Earth from space. Some set photography goals, like taking a picture of every Major League Baseball stadium in the United States or each of the "wonders of the world."

With no gravity in space, it's very easy to lose things. It just takes a small bump and objects can go flying, finding nooks and crannies they can disappear into for days at a time. Mission Control even sends up notes asking astronauts to be on the lookout for various pieces of equipment. One camera lens was lost for years! It was finally found behind a rack that hadn't been moved in ages.

Playing with food in space is absolutely allowed! It's a whole lot of fun and is a wonderful way to celebrate the effects of living without gravity with the rest of the team. Care must be taken though. If the food makes a lot of crumbs, it's best to be close to an air vent that can help suck the particles into a filter. We'll vacuum it later!

NASA hopes to be able to grow food in the spaceships that will make the long journey to Mars someday. Growing plants without dirt is something quite new to most earthlings, who have been planting seeds in soil for centuries. Special lighting is used to make the veggies grow faster and stronger in outer space.

Astronauts go to food tastings before blastoff. They taste every food available and give each one a rating from 1 to 10 (10 is good!). The ground team then prepares each astronaut's personal menu considering calories, variety, and meal type (breakfast, lunch, and dinner). When astronauts score a food 7 or higher, they will see it on their menu in space!

Living and working in space is a wild change. Everything that comes naturally on Earth is completely different without gravity. Using tools, writing, typing on a computer—even sleeping presents a whole new experience. And while we really don't need our legs much, our feet become more like an extra pair of hands—they're especially useful for sticking under a handrail to help keep us steady as we move around the ship!

Teamwork is a key component of spaceflight. While astronauts may be the ones who fly in outer space, there are hundreds of amazing folks on the ground who work countless hours keeping the crew and their spacecraft safe. When the team on Earth says "failure is not an option," it means they know the astronauts are counting on them to solve any problem we face! Spaceflight is the ultimate team sport!

To my family . . .
and to every other family in the Universe.
Keep turning pages into dreams.

—Clayton

*

To Robert who loves me to the Space Station and back.

—Susan

Text Copyright © 2020 Clayton Anderson
Illustration Copyright © 2020 Susan Batori
Design Copyright © 2020 Sleeping Bear Press

All rights reserved. No part of this book may be reproduced in any manner
without the express written consent of the publisher, except in the case of brief
excerpts in critical reviews and articles. All inquiries should be addressed to:

SLEEPING BEAR PRESS™

2395 South Huron Parkway, Suite 200
Ann Arbor, MI 48104
www.sleepingbearpress.com

Printed and bound in China.

Library of Congress Cataloging-in-Publication Data

Names: Anderson, Clayton C., 1959- author. | Batori, Susan, illustrator.
Title: Letters from space / by Clayton Anderson ; illustrated by Susan Batori.
Description: Ann Arbor, Michigan : Sleeping Bear Press, [2020] | Audience:
Ages 4-8. | Summary: "Astronaut Clayton Anderson lived aboard the
International Space Station—and while he didn't mail letters home,
imagine if he did! These letters are full of weird science, wild facts,
and outrageous true stories from life in space. Backmatter includes even
more information on space, astronauts, and living among the stars"—
Provided by publisher.
Identifiers: LCCN 2020007406 | ISBN 9781534110748 (hardcover)
Subjects: CYAC: Astronauts—Fiction. | Letters—Fiction. | International
Space Station—Fiction.
Classification: LCC PZ7.1.A52 Let 2020 | DDC [E]—dc23
LC record available at https://lccn.loc.gov/2020007406